This Little Tiger book belongs to:

_____

_____

_____

For Mea and Edison
- S C

For S P, the man who loves to build beautiful things
- C P

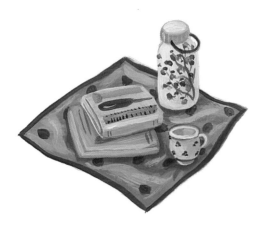

LITTLE TIGER PRESS LTD.
an imprint of the Little Tiger Group
1 Coda Studios, 189 Munster Road, London SW6 6AW
www.littletiger.co.uk
First published in Great Britain 2016
This edition published 2016
Text by Suzanne Chiew
Text copyright © Little Tiger Press 2016
Illustrations copyright © Caroline Pedler 2016

Caroline Pedler has asserted her right to be
identified as the illustrator of this work under
the Copyright, Designs and Patents Act, 1988

A CIP catalogue record for this book is available from the British Library

Printed in China • LTP/2700/2561/1018

4 6 8 10 9 7 5 3

Badger AND THE Great RESCUE

Suzanne Chiew • Caroline Pedler

LITTLE TIGER

LONDON

One bright day, Badger was busy reading
when Mouse raced up.

"Badger, look at this rope I've found!" she cried.
"It's perfect for a washing line. Will you help
me make one?"

"Of course!" smiled Badger.

He picked up his tool bag and off
they went.

In no time at all, Mouse's washing hung on her brand new line.

"I wonder where the rope came from?" said Badger. Then something in the bushes caught his eye. He reached into the leaves and heaved it out.

"It's a basket!" squeaked Mouse. "It's a mystery!" frowned Badger. "How ever did it get here?"

Mouse hopped excitedly. "It would make a brilliant shed for Hedgehog!"
Badger nodded. "Let's surprise him."

They patched and mended until the shed was perfect.
"Hedgehog will be so pleased!" Mouse giggled. And she was right!

"Thank you!" squealed Hedgehog. "It's wonderful!"
"We found it in the bushes," said Mouse.
"That's strange," said Hedgehog. "I've found
something too. Come with me."

But when they reached the clearing,
Rabbit was already there.

"Look at my lovely cloth!" he cried.
"I'm going to make a tent."

"But I need it to make a hammock!"
said Hedgehog.

"Can I have some for a kite?"
Mouse asked.

"We can share it," smiled Badger.
"There's plenty to go around."

Rabbit carefully divided
up the cloth.

"Hold on!" frowned Hedgehog.
"Why have you got the
biggest piece?"

"Because I'm the biggest," said Rabbit.

"But I found it first!" huffed Hedgehog.

"And my piece is too small to make anything!" Mouse sniffed.

The friends started to bicker, and soon there was a terrible rumpus.

"STOP!" called Badger. "There's no need to squabble. We can share the cloth equally. Look."

He divided the cloth into three equal pieces.

"Hooray!" everyone cheered.

"I'll start snipping," beamed Rabbit.
But just then Bird swooped down.
"Quick, quick!" she chirped.
"Someone needs our help!"

They followed Bird to the tallest tree in the forest. There, clinging to a branch, was a frightened little mole.

"Help!" he yelled. "HELP!"
"How terrible!" fretted Rabbit.
"What can we do?" squeaked Mouse.
Badger frowned. "We must rescue him!"

"I could try to lift him down," offered Bird. "But I think he'll be too heavy."

"We could build a really tall ladder!" Hedgehog suggested. "But that would take a very long time."

"I know!" said Rabbit. "Mole can jump and we'll catch him in that piece of cloth!"
They all rushed off to get it.

The friends stretched out the cloth like a huge trampoline.
"Jump, Mole!" shouted Badger.
"We'll catch you!"

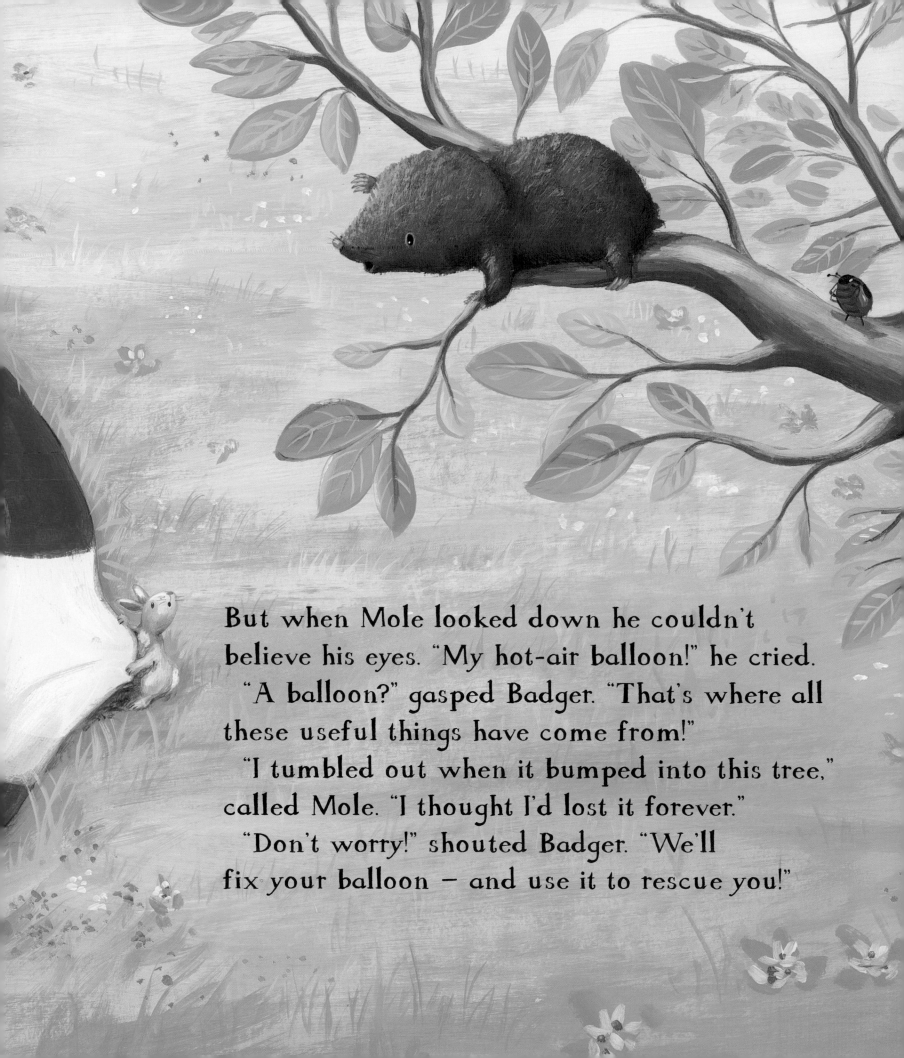

But when Mole looked down he couldn't believe his eyes. "My hot-air balloon!" he cried.

"A balloon?" gasped Badger. "That's where all these useful things have come from!"

"I tumbled out when it bumped into this tree," called Mole. "I thought I'd lost it forever."

"Don't worry!" shouted Badger. "We'll fix your balloon – and use it to rescue you!"

"I'm sorry there'll be no new washing line or shed," said Badger as they collected the pieces of Mole's balloon.
"We don't mind," the friends replied.
"We must help Mole!"

Everyone set to work.
They knotted and tied,

and stitched and glued,

until the balloon was
as good as new.

"We're coming, Mole!" called Rabbit as the balloon sailed up, up, upwards.

At the top of the tree, Badger reached out with a strong, friendly paw. "Don't be frightened, Mole," he said. "Just hold on tight."

"You won't let go?" whispered Mole.
"I promise," said Badger.
And with a WHOOSH, he pulled
Mole to safety.

"What lovely new friends you are!"
beamed Mole. "How can I ever thank you?"
   "Well—" said Badger.
   "We were hoping you'd take us for a ride!"
laughed Rabbit.
   "That's a wonderful idea!" giggled Mole.
"Away we go!"
   And they all floated off towards
a brand new adventure.

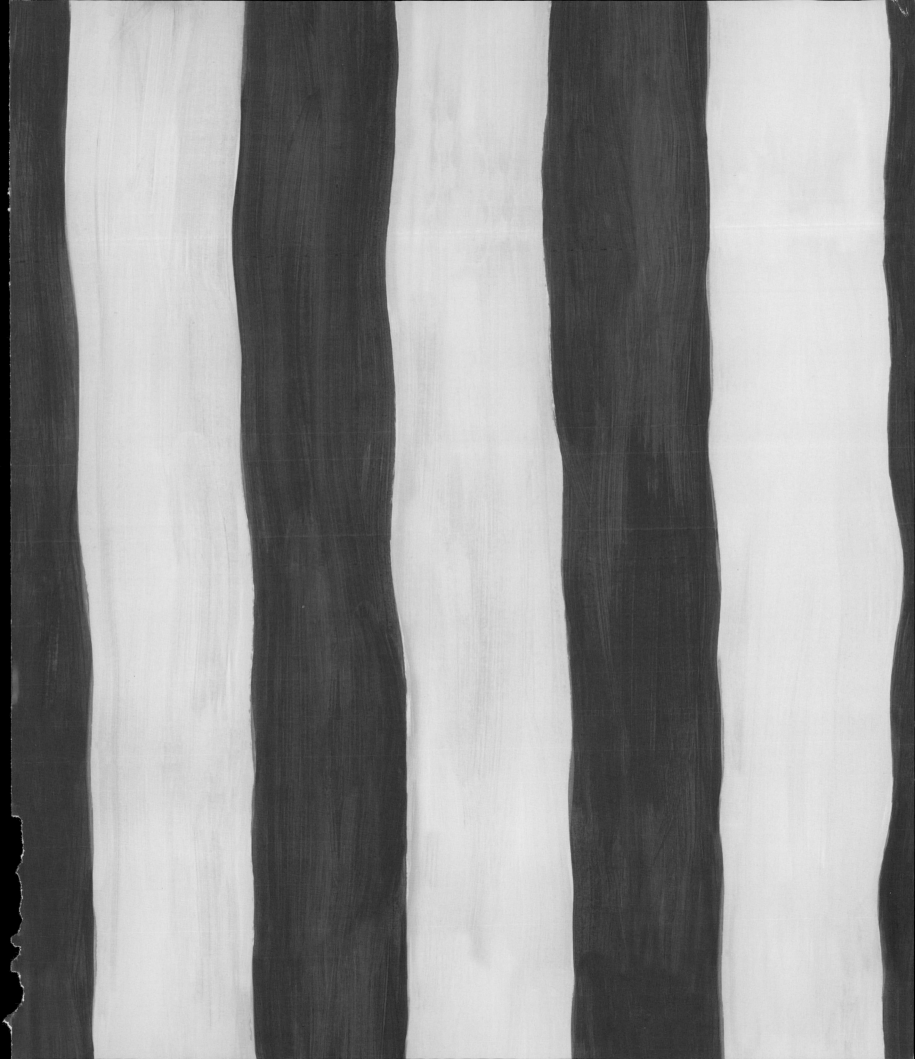